Follow My Leader!

EMMA CHICHESTER CLARK

Collins

An imprint of HarperCollins*Publishers*

for Finn

Have you read these picture books by Emma Chichester Clark?
The Glove Puppet Man - written by John Yeoman
More!
I Love You, Blue Kangaroo!

And watch out for:
Where Are You, Blue Kangaroo?

First published in hardback in Great Britain by Andersen Press Ltd in 1999
First published in Picture Lions in 2001
1 3 5 7 9 10 8 6 4 2
ISBN: 0 00 664760 X
Picture Lions is an imprint of the Children's Division, part of HarperCollins Publishers Ltd.
Text and illustrations copyright © Emma Chichester Clark 1999
The author/illustrator asserts the moral right to be identified as the author/illustrator of the work.
A CIP catalogue record for this title is available from the British Library.
The HarperCollins website address is: www.fireandwater.com
Printed and bound in Hong Kong

Along the path,
Hopping and skipping,
Follow my leader!

Through the trees,
Whirling and twirling,
Follow my leader!

Over the stile,
Leaping and bounding,
Follow my leader!

Up the hill,
Puffing and panting,
Follow my leader!

Round the corner,
Jumping and jiving,
Follow my leader!

Down the steps,
Bumping and thumping,
Follow my leader!

Across the stream,
Splishing and splashing,
Follow my leader!

Into the woods,
Shouting and roaring,
Follow my leader!

But wait . . .
Can you hear it?
Shhh! What's that noise?

"I want to play,"
The tiger said, smiling.

"Well," said the boy,
"Just let me see . . ."

"All right," he said slowly,
"You are the leader,
But the rules of the game are . . .
You MUSTN'T turn round!"

The tiger roared,
"READY?"

Out of the woods,
Shouting and roaring,
Follow my leader!

Across the stream,
Splishing and splashing,
Follow my leader!

Up the steps,
Bumping and thumping,
Follow my leader!

Round the corner,
Jumping and jiving,
Follow my leader!

Down the hill,
Puffing and panting,
Follow my leader!

Over the stile,
Leaping and bounding,
Follow my leader!

Through the trees,
Whirling and twirling,
Follow my leader!

Up the path,
Skipping and hopping,
Follow my leader!

Through the gate,
Quickly and quietly,
Follow my leader!

Close the door,
Grinning and gasping,
Follow my leader!

See him go,
Dancing and prancing,
Follow my leader,
Follow my leader,
Follow my leader,
RRROOOAAR!